ABClimb

Words & Pictures by

Bridgett Ross

To my son Emmitt:
Climb on!

A

Anchor

B

Belay

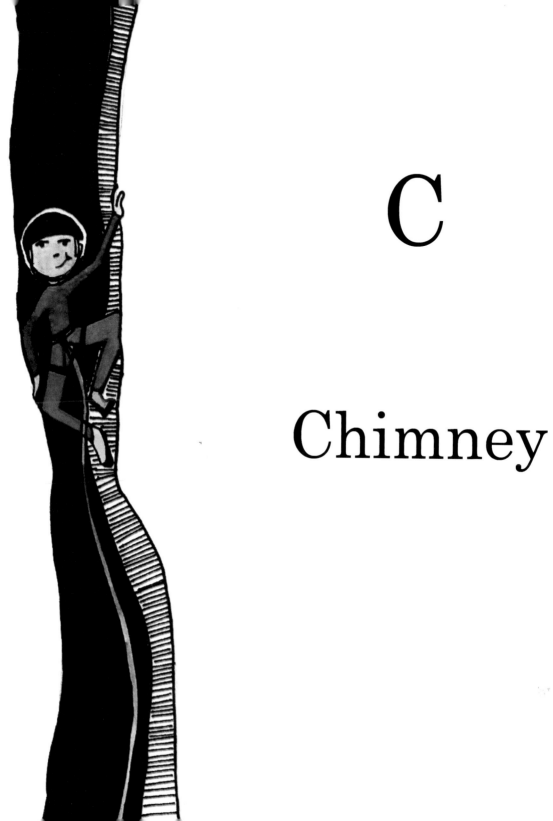

C

Chimney

D

Dyno

E

Edging

F

Finger Crack

G

Glove

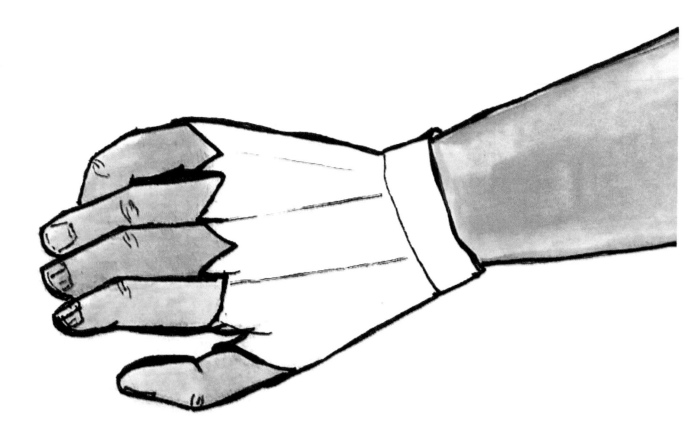

H

Helmet

I

Indoor Climbing

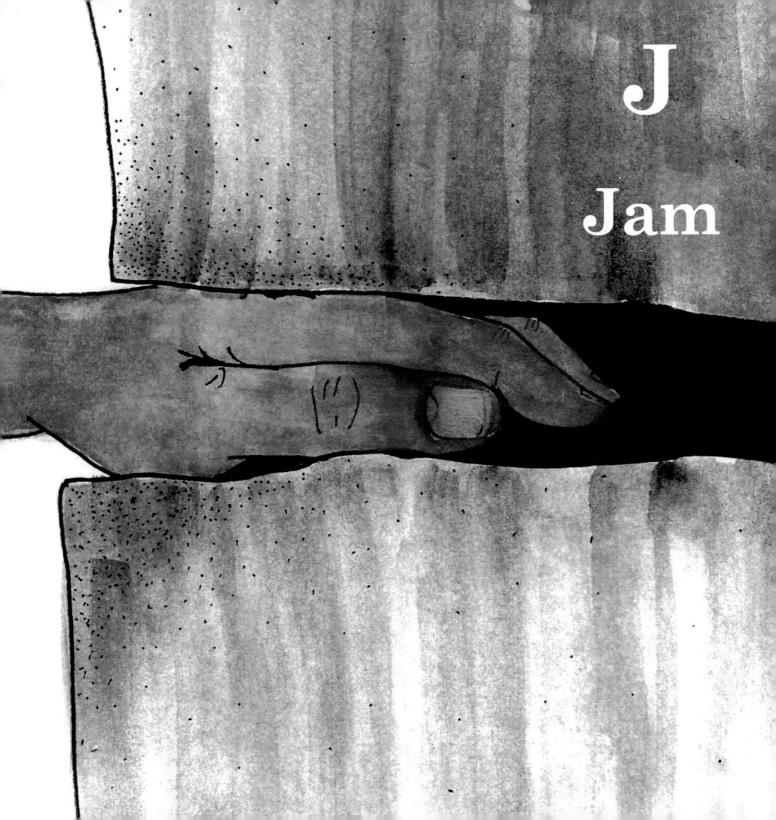

J

Jam

K

Knot

L

Lieback

M

Mantle

N

Nut

O
Offwidth

P

Piton

Q

Quickdraw

R

Rock climber

S

Stemming

T

Top rope

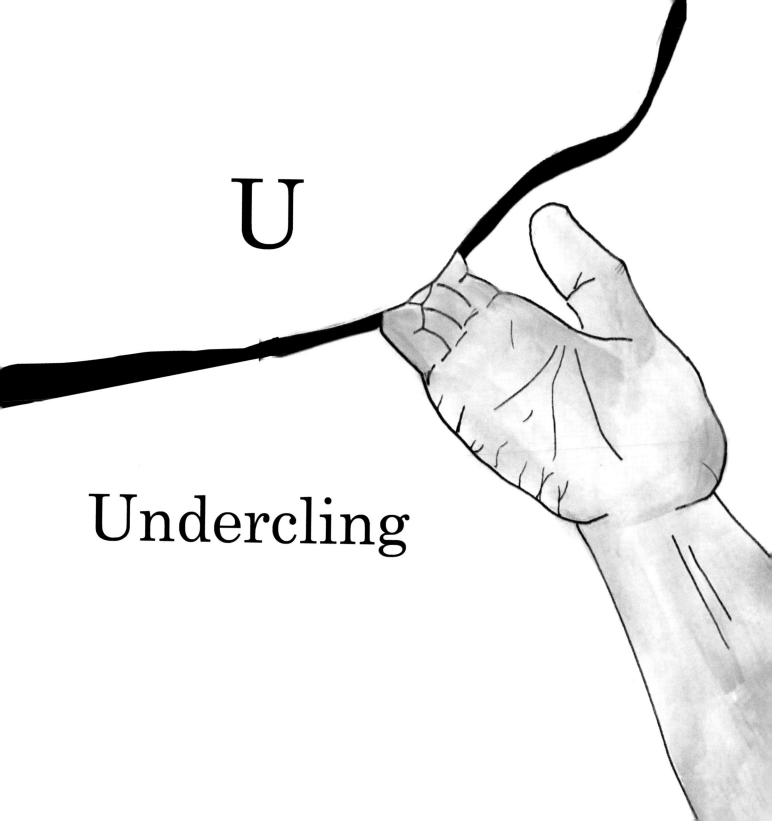

U

Undercling

V
Van Life

W

Webbing

X

Sliding X

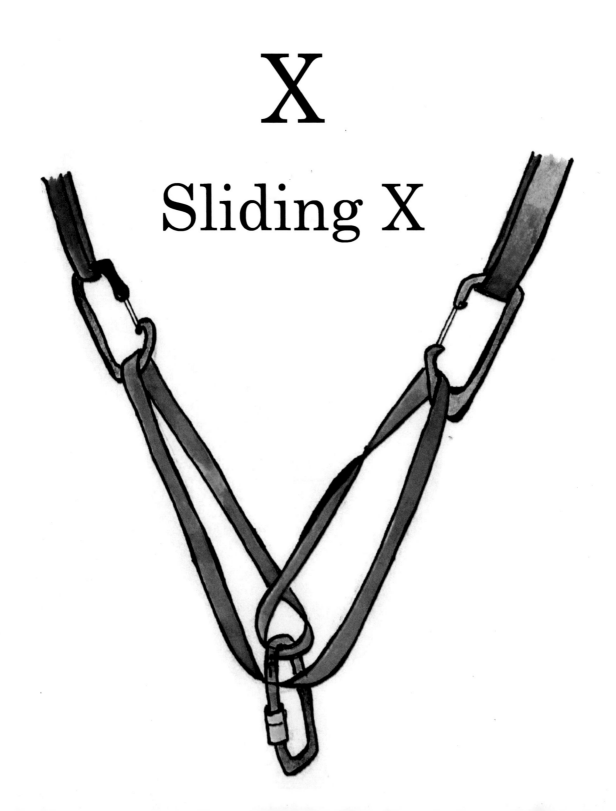

Y

Yosemite

Z

Z-clip

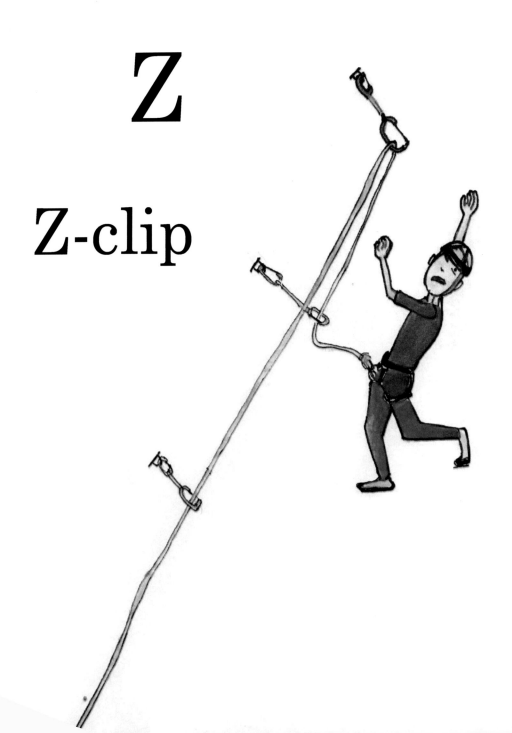

Made in the USA
Middletown, DE
20 May 2020